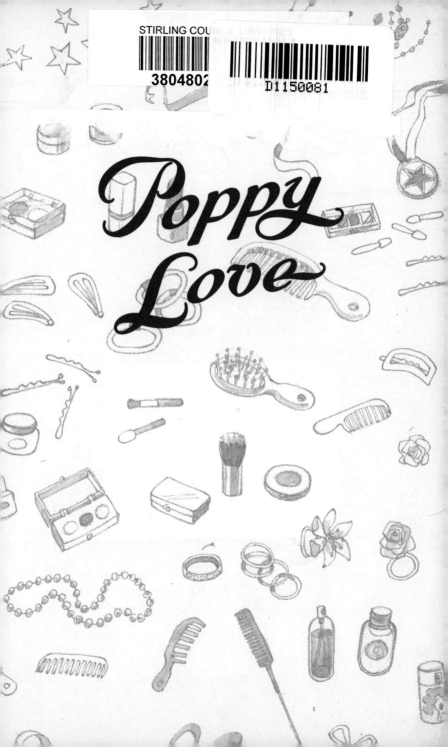

Poppy Love

Poppy Love titles

Poppy Love Steps Out

Poppy Love Faces the Music

Poppy Love Rock 'n' Roll

Poppy Love Star Turn

Poppy Love
Faces the Music

NATASHA MAY

illustrated by
SHELAGH McNICHOLAS

WALKER
BOOKS

*With thanks to Neil Kelly and the students of
Rubies Dance Centre
N.M.*

*With thanks to Carolyn, Julia, Kirsty and Ann at
Bell's Dance Centre
S.N.*

First published 2009 by Walker Books Ltd
87 Vauxhall Walk, London SE11 5HJ

2 4 6 8 10 9 7 5 3 1

Text © 2009 Veronica Bennett
Illustrations © 2009 Shelagh McNicholas

The author and illustrator have asserted their moral rights
in accordance with the Copyright, Designs and Patents Act 1988

This book has been typeset in ITC Giovanni

Printed and bound in Great Britain by Clays Ltd, St Ives plc

British Library Cataloguing in Publication Data:
a catalogue record for this book is available from the British Library

ISBN 978-1-4063-1134-1

www.walker.co.uk

Contents

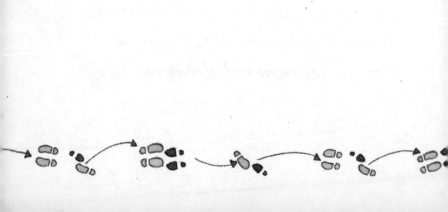

Feed the Birds

Poppy Love loved ballroom dancing.

She went to Miss Johnson's classes every week at the Blue Horizon Dance Studio, and already had medals to show she had passed dancing tests.

On Fridays at six o'clock Poppy and her partner, Zack Bishop, had Miss Johnson all to themselves for a whole hour's lesson. Poppy really enjoyed these sessions. She and

Zack could dance across the empty floor, and round it, and right into the corners without getting in anyone's way. It made Poppy feel like a ballroom dancing star on TV!

As they whirled round to the lilting music of the waltz, or jumped and kicked in a lively jive, she would imagine herself in tights and a short, spangled skirt or an ankle-length gown. Beside her in the mirror she could see Zack waltzing in a jacket with tails at the back or jiving in a suit sprinkled with sequins. Of course, what the mirror *really* reflected was Poppy in an old top and loose skirt, and Zack in tracksuit bottoms and a white T-shirt with *Blue Horizon Dance Studio* printed on it. They were still in the juvenile section of ballroom dancing competitions and were too young for long dresses or coat-tails. But Poppy could dream, and she *did*.

Each week at seven o'clock, Poppy was always sorry the lesson was over, and she began to look forward to the next one. But one Friday, the clock on the studio wall said only six minutes to seven when Miss Johnson went to the CD player and stopped the music. "That's enough for tonight," she said.

Her brown eyes followed Poppy's blue ones to the clock. "It's all right, Poppy," she said, "you're not going home yet. I just want to talk to you for a minute."

She folded her arms and looked at Poppy and Zack with her head to one side. "You two really enjoyed doing the South East Juvenile Ballroom Dancing Competition last month, didn't you?"

Poppy and Zack *had* enjoyed their very first competition. They had danced lots of dances, with each other and with some of Miss Johnson's other pupils. Poppy remembered how the children had cheered one another on. Although she and Zack hadn't won anything, it had been such a fun day Poppy hadn't wanted it to end.

"It was great," she said. "We can't wait to do another one, can we, Zack?"

Miss Johnson smiled. "Even if it's a more important competition this time, and needs a lot of practice?"

"We don't mind," said Zack eagerly. "We'll work as hard as we can."

"Good." Miss Johnson was pleased. "Because I want to enter you in the South East Regional Championships."

Poppy's heart seemed to turn over. Entering the Regionals would mean dancing against more couples than ever before. It wouldn't just be children from around the town of Brighton, where Poppy and Zack lived, but a large area that included London. And as London was such a huge city, it must have *loads* of good couples.

"If you get through to the semi-final in any of the events," Miss Johnson went on, "it means you can enter that event in the Nationwide Finals next year."

Poppy swallowed, looking at Zack. On his

face was surprise, but also pride. "Let's do it!" he said to Miss Johnson. Then he turned to Poppy. "You want to, don't you, Pop?"

"Just try and stop me!" replied Poppy.

It was seven o'clock. "I'll speak to your parents about extra lessons next time," said Miss Johnson. "You'd better get going now."

Poppy wondered if there was any time left in the week for extra lessons. She already did a class with all Miss Johnson's other ballroom dancing children on Saturday mornings, and the more advanced Competition Class after school on Wednesdays. It was fun, but hard work.

Outside the studio, Zack's mother was the only one waiting. "Oh heavens," she said anxiously when she saw Poppy. "Am I supposed to pick you up tonight?"

"No, my auntie's coming," Poppy told her. "She's probably just late."

"I don't see her car," said Mrs Bishop, looking around. "I hope she comes soon. Zack and I have got to go to the station."

"My gran's bringing my cousin Anna to stay," explained Zack. "Maybe you'll meet Anna while she's here."

"Does she like dancing?" Poppy asked.

"Yes," said Zack, "but she's got a wheelchair."

"Anna was born with a bad back, and she's unable to walk," explained Mrs Bishop. "But she does love dancing, and music too. She lives in Birmingham, which is a long way from the coast, so it'll be nice for her to come to the seaside for a week."

Poppy was just wondering what it must

be like not to be able to walk when a car she didn't recognize drew up. Her Auntie Jill wound down the window and waved from the passenger seat. "Thanks for waiting!" she called to Mrs Bishop.

"Isn't that Simon driving?" Zack asked Poppy.

Poppy looked into the car and nodded.

"Nice wheels," said Zack, looking enviously at the large silver car.

Simon Forrester was Auntie Jill's new boyfriend. They had met only a few weeks before, but since then Poppy's aunt had been several times to Forrester's, the restaurant Simon owned. She'd gone out with him to other places, too, and at home she'd begun to talk about him a lot. Poppy's older brother Tom liked to tease his aunt, rolling his eyes and putting "Simon says!" before everything she said.

Mrs Bishop and Zack went to meet Anna's train, and Poppy got in Simon's car.

"Can you guess where Simon and I have been today?" Auntie Jill asked.

"New York?" said Poppy, who was feeling in a silly mood.

Simon laughed. "I wish!"

"Seriously," said Auntie Jill. "We were at a tea dance."

"What's a tea dance?" asked Poppy in surprise. Drinking tea and dancing didn't seem to go together. You certainly couldn't do them both at the same time.

"You sit at a table and have tea and cakes," explained Simon.

"And there's a band playing, and you get up and dance."

"It was in the ballroom on the pier, and it was so much fun!" went on Auntie Jill enthusiastically. "They hold it every Friday afternoon. So would you and Zack like to come with us next Friday? It's the last week of the holidays." She whispered behind her hand. "I'm teaching Simon to dance, you see. He's … well, he's getting better, but he needs the practice."

Auntie Jill used to be a ballroom dancing champion, and she still worked as a judge for competitions and medal tests. Now she and Poppy's mum ran the Hotel Gemini. She seemed quite happy living in the flat at the top of the hotel with the Love family, but Poppy knew she missed her dancing days very much.

"I'm trying really hard," said Simon to Poppy. "Jill tells me you and Zack are wonderful dancers."

When Simon said this a warm feeling came over Poppy, like when she got out of the bath and wrapped herself in a towel that had been on the radiator.

"How was your lesson?" asked Auntie Jill.

"Good," answered Poppy. "Miss Johnson's going to enter us for the Regionals." She couldn't help sounding proud of herself.

She hoped Simon wouldn't think she was showing off.

"Wow!" exclaimed Auntie Jill. "That's a qualifying event for the Nationwide Finals," she told Simon.

Simon grinned at Poppy in the rear-view mirror. "Well done, Poppy. And Zack, too. Best of luck."

"Thanks," said Poppy. The word luck always made her think about Lucky, her toy puppy, who sometimes brought her luck and sometimes didn't. "We'll need it."

When Simon dropped
them outside the hotel,
Poppy followed her aunt
up the wide steps. As
they opened the door
and heard the little bell
ring, Poppy had her Big

Idea. She was so excited that she tripped over
the doormat, and only just managed to stop
herself tumbling into the hall.

"Auntie Jill!" She caught hold of her aunt's
arm. "Could we take someone else to the tea
dance too?"

"Of course, but who?" asked her aunt,
looking mystified.

"Anna."

Auntie Jill had heard all about Anna from
Mrs Bishop. "That's a lovely idea!"

Suddenly, Poppy thought of something. "Won't Anna mind that she can't join in the dancing?"

"Maybe she can," said Auntie Jill. "After all, she plays in a wheelchair netball team. And there are wheelchair ballroom dancing clubs, too."

Poppy felt better. "I can't wait for Friday!" she said.

"I'll phone Mrs Bishop tomorrow," said Auntie Jill, laughing.

When Simon stopped his car at Zack's house, he and his mum were waiting outside on the pavement. Beside them sat a girl a little older than Zack.

Simon and Auntie Jill lifted Anna into the back seat, next to Poppy, and Mrs Bishop folded the wheelchair and put it in the boot of the car.

"And before you ask, Zack," joked Auntie Jill, "yes, you can ride in the front!"

Zack scrambled into the front seat, grinning, and they set off.

"Anna, this is Poppy," he said to his cousin.

"I guessed it was," said Anna, giving Poppy a "boys!" look. "This is so nice, isn't it, going to a tea dance?" She glanced at Poppy's blue dance dress. "Did I wear the right thing?"

Poppy thought Anna's patterned skirt and pink top were lovely. "You look great," she said, ignoring Zack's "girls!" look.

When they went into the ballroom on the pier, Anna's brown eyes widened. "It's beautiful!" she exclaimed.

At one end of the large room was a raised platform decorated with plants like palm trees, growing in pots. A pianist, a drummer and a guitarist in maroon jackets and bow ties were playing dance music. All around the edges of the floor were little tables, each with a white tablecloth and a small vase of flowers. People were sitting at some of the tables, and several couples were already on the dance floor.

Anna, Poppy and Zack were the only children there. A tea dance was obviously a very grown-up occasion, not interesting to most children. But Poppy and Zack weren't

like most children. They were probably the best dancers in the room. Zack's face plainly said, "Come on, Pop!"

The band was playing a waltz tune Poppy knew well. It was "Feed the Birds" from *Mary Poppins.*

"I love this song," said Anna, and began to sing the words softly.

As Zack led Poppy onto the floor, she knew people were looking at them. When she heard Simon say to Auntie Jill, "Do they really prefer dancing to food?" she smiled to herself. She *did* prefer dancing to food. She preferred it to everything!

One-two-three, *one*-two-three went the waltz music. Round and round went the dancers. Poppy was enjoying herself, as she always did when she danced. But today was special. Anna's big smile showed that she was glad to be there. Dancing was like that. It made people happy.

"Now, Simon," said Auntie Jill when Poppy and Zack got back to the table. "Your turn!"

The children watched as Simon took Auntie Jill in the correct hold and held his head up confidently. He waited for the beat of the music, then began the dance on the correct foot.

"He's quite good," said Zack thoughtfully.

"She's *very* good, though," said Anna.

"She used to be a champion," Poppy told her. "Until her

partner got married to someone else."

Zack raised his eyebrows. "I wonder…"

As the children ate their tea, Poppy looked at Simon and her aunt dancing together, and wondered too what the future held. Then Anna touched Zack's arm and said something unexpected.

"Will you dance with me, Zack?"

Zack was surprised, but very pleased. He got up and stood by Anna's wheelchair.

"And you too, Poppy," said Anna shyly. "We can all dance together."

But just as they got to the middle of the dance floor, the music ended and the dancers applauded. "Oh no!" said Anna, disappointed.

Before Poppy could change her mind, she
went to the edge of the band's platform.
"Please would you play 'Feed the Birds'
again?" she asked the man at the piano. "My
friend really likes that tune."

The piano man gave a little nod to the
other musicians. "We'll be happy to," he said
with a smile.

"Thank you," said Poppy.

"And thank *you*, Poppy!" said Anna,
holding out her hands to Poppy and Zack.
"Now, if you're ready, let's dance!"

Surprise!

It was the first day of the new school year.
Poppy had butterflies in her stomach as she
picked up the cereal packet and put it down
again. She didn't really want any breakfast.

A smartly dressed boy appeared at the
door of the kitchen. Dad, who was gulping
his second cup of tea, stared. "Poppy, do you
recognize this boy?" he asked.

"Oh, *Dad*." Poppy poured a very little bit

of cereal into her bowl and climbed onto a stool. It was only Tom in his new uniform.

Tom had more reason than Poppy to have butterflies. He was starting secondary school today. But he took a large portion of cereal and smothered it with milk and sugar. He also took an apple from the fruit bowl and put it in the pocket of his new blazer.

Dad finished his tea, kissed Poppy and patted Tom's shoulder. "Have a good day," he said, picking up his briefcase. "I'll have to run or I'll miss my train. See you two later."

When Dad had gone, Poppy watched Tom shovelling cereal into his mouth. "Don't you feel sick?" she asked.

"Why should I?"

"Aren't you nervous? Everything's going to be new at school."

"Don't worry, Pop, it'll be cool."

One of the things Poppy liked about her brother was that he was always cheerful. Even if he got cross for a moment, as everyone does, he'd forget it in an instant.

His spoon clattered into his empty bowl. "I'd better go," he said, climbing off his stool. "Mustn't be late on the first day."

Tom was going to school on the bus alone. Mum had wanted to go with him on the first day, but to Tom that was definitely *not* cool. "Mum, I'm almost twelve!" he'd protested.

When he'd gone, Poppy picked up another spoonful of cereal. She'd just put it in her mouth when Mum came into the kitchen and sat down next to her. "Listen, Poppy," she said. "You know it's Tom's birthday on Saturday?"

Poppy nodded, swallowing her mouthful.

"Well, Dad and I want to give him a surprise."

"A present?" asked Poppy, forgetting all about feeling nervous.

"A sort of present," said Mum. "Not a thing, but an event."

"A party!"

"That's right," said Mum. "A proper grown-up party, downstairs in the hotel."

"Oh, Mum, he'll love that!" Poppy was so excited she bounced up and down on the stool. For his birthday last year, Tom and his friends had gone tenpin bowling, then eaten at a pizza restaurant.

No girls had been invited, even Poppy. But a grown-up party wasn't a grown-up party without girls as well as boys, was it?

"Can Mia come?" asked Poppy eagerly. "She *is* my best friend, and Tom knows her, doesn't he? And Zack, of course?"

"I expect so!" said Mum, laughing. "But listen, Poppy. The party is a surprise, so we've got to decorate the room, set up the disco and the lights, and prepare the food – all in secret!"

"How will we keep Tom out of the way?"

"He and Dad are going on a boat trip on Saturday afternoon. You know how crazy they are about boats!" Mum rolled her eyes. "Look, why don't we go to town after school this afternoon and get some party decorations?"

"That would be fun!"
Poppy drank the last
of her juice and put
her backpack over her
shoulders. "Can Mia come

round early on Saturday, so we can get ready
for the party together?"

Mum smiled. "Of course, if she doesn't
mind helping to blow up about a hundred
balloons!"

"A party!" Mia clapped her hands. "Cool!"

Mia had been visiting her mum's relations
in China all summer, so she and Poppy had
lots of news for each other. As soon as the
bell went for morning break, they ran out
and sat in the shade of the linden tree on the
school field.

"There's going to be a disco," Poppy told her friend. "And a hundred balloons, and—"

"Soppy Poppy Love!" shouted a boy's voice. "Got your sparkly shoes on? And where's your suntan? Came off in the rain, did it?"

Ryan Buxton was always making fun of Poppy's dancing. To him it was a big joke. He also thought it was funny that Poppy's family couldn't go on holiday in the summer like a lot of families because they owned a hotel.

Poppy and Mia knew the only way to deal with him was to ignore him, so they went on talking as if nothing had happened. Ryan stared at them rudely for a moment, then ran off.

"I went on a huge aeroplane," Mia told Poppy. "And everything was so different in China. Mum's teaching me to do Chinese writing." Her dark eyes looked at Poppy brightly. "What did *you* do in the summer, Poppy?"

"Well, I didn't go on any aeroplanes," said Poppy. "But I did learn to do cartwheels!"

"That's great!" said Mia, who was one of the best gymnasts in Brighton. She held up her hand for a high-five. "You'll be doing gymnastics like me next!"

Poppy slapped Mia's hand, laughing. "Will you come round to my house on Saturday afternoon, and bring your party things, and we'll get dressed for the party together? You can do my hair and I'll do yours. It'll be brilliant!"

Everything was ready. The disco equipment had been set up

on the low stage at one end
of the room. At the other
end there was a table covered
with party food, a large cake
in the shape of a football pitch
taking pride of place. Poppy and Mia had
helped Mum hang up bunches of balloons,
while Auntie Jill had fixed silver and gold
streamers all around the stage. Above it, a
HAPPY BIRTHDAY TOM! banner twinkled under
the coloured lights.

Guests began to arrive. Poppy watched as
Tom's friends came in, wearing their best
clothes and carrying presents and cards. Mia
was beside her, looking very excited, and
Zack appeared with gelled hair and new
jeans. As seven o'clock approached,
Mum went to the microphone.

"Right, everyone," she said, "Tom's going to be here any minute, so let's hide!"

They all crouched down behind tables and chairs, trying not to giggle. From her hiding place Poppy heard Mum phone Dad and say "All clear!" Then she nodded to Auntie Jill. "Lights off, please!"

Poppy's heart beat very fast as they waited in the dark. Suppose, in spite of everything they'd done, Tom had found out about the party? She knew Tom would pretend to be surprised, even if he wasn't. But it wouldn't be the same. She crossed her fingers.

Then she heard Dad's voice in the hallway, and the door opened.

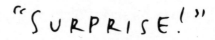

"SURPRISE!"

All of a sudden the lights went on, and everyone jumped out from their hiding places, yelling and clapping. In the doorway, with his mouth open in an "O" shape and his eyebrows nearly in his hair, stood Tom. Poppy couldn't help laughing. He was surprised all right!

"Awesome!" he said as soon as he could make himself heard over the noise.

Tom's friends gathered excitedly round him. "Come and open your presents!" they urged. But before they could pull Tom away, he turned to his family, pleased but puzzled. "How did you do all this without me finding out?" he asked.

"Your mum and I invited everyone by phoning their parents when you were at school," explained Auntie Jill. "And Poppy kept you out of the kitchen this morning while Chef finished icing the cake and getting the food ready."

"And I thought you really *did* want to play Monopoly!" said Tom to Poppy. He was smiling a big smile. "Did you let me win on purpose?"

"Of course," said Poppy. "It's your birthday!"

"I had the easy job," Dad told Tom, "taking you out on a boat. Though every time Mum rang my mobile, I had to remember just to answer yes or no, so as not to give the game away."

Tom laughed. "I never suspected a

thing. I thought Mum just wanted to gossip!"

"Cheeky boy!" said Mum.

The DJ had put on a hit song everyone knew well, with a strong drumbeat and a good tune. Poppy couldn't wait to start dancing. She took Zack's hand to pull him onto the floor. But he pulled back. "No one else is ready to dance yet, Pop," he said. "And we'd look stupid out there on our own. It'd be like a demonstration, not a disco."

He was right. The music was playing, the coloured lights were spinning, but most of the boys and girls had gathered round Tom, who was opening his presents. Others were at the table, eating and chatting and laughing. They looked as if they were having a good time, but no one seemed to want to dance.

Twenty minutes, then half an hour passed. Eventually Auntie Jill took Poppy's hand and they danced together, trying to encourage others to join in. But although the party guests stood around the edges of the room, some of the girls swaying in time to the beat, or singing the words, no one danced. Poppy couldn't even persuade Zack, who was busy trying out Tom's new games console, to come onto the floor.

"What's the matter with them?" Poppy whispered to her aunt. "The music's so great, and they look as if they *want* to dance, but they won't."

"Maybe they're shy," suggested Auntie Jill. She looked at her watch. "But if the dancing doesn't start soon, the party will be over. It isn't much of a disco, I'm afraid!"

Poppy was disappointed, but was sure people *would* dance, if only they would let themselves go. Looking round the room, she caught sight of Mia, who waved. Suddenly, Poppy thought of something.

"Mia!" she called, hurrying towards her friend. "I've got an idea!"

Surprised, Mia allowed Poppy to take her out into the corridor. "Now," said Poppy, "watch what I do, and copy me. We'll soon turn this party into a disco!"

When they went back in the floor was still empty, and Zack was still in the huddle of game-playing boys. Poppy asked the DJ to put on a song she was sure everyone would love. Then she and Mia stood side by side in front of the stage.

"OK, everybody, follow us!" called Poppy.

At first the guests just watched as she and Mia began to dance the steps they'd worked out – easy, fun steps that anyone could follow, while the rhythm of the music boomed loudly. But slowly, shyly, then more boldly, people began to line up behind the girls and copy their steps.

Zack, to Poppy's relief, was one of the first to join in. But the other boys soon found they couldn't resist the beat of the drums and the stamping, turning steps. Soon, the only people left at the side of the room were the grown-ups.

"Look at Tom," Dad said to Mum in amazement. "He's *dancing*!"

Poppy looked at her brother too. He wasn't only dancing, he was having a lot of fun. And so were his friends. Even boys who normally thought dancing was only for girls!

"Ryan Buxton should be here!" Poppy called to Mia over the music "Wouldn't you love to see him dancing!"

"Yes, I would," replied Mia, starting to giggle. "I'm glad he's not here, though! He's so rude!"

"But nobody can be rude and dance at the same time," said Poppy. "So if I could get Ryan to dance, do you think it would make him a bit nicer?"

"In your dreams, Pop!" replied Mia, still giggling, and danced away.

The room got hot. People took off their sweatshirts and cardigans and left them on the backs of chairs. For now, Tom had forgotten all about his presents, even the new games console. Poppy looked round at the crowd of shiny, smiling faces and felt very happy that the party had turned into a proper disco after all.

"Poppy!" she heard her brother call behind her. When she turned round, he was standing with his hands on his hips, looking very hot and grinning at her. "This disco is the *best*!" he said.

Cold Feet

One Saturday morning Poppy woke up early and started to get out of bed to go to dance class. Then she remembered that this Saturday was different.

"The Regional Championships are next weekend," Miss Johnson had told Poppy's mum and Mrs Bishop at the end of last night's lesson. "So instead of their usual class tomorrow morning, I'd like Poppy and Zack to do a dress rehearsal of their competition dances at three o'clock in the afternoon."

"Make-up and hair too?" Mum had asked.

"Of course," Miss Johnson had said, smiling and tidying a strand of shiny dark hair behind Poppy's ear. "And I think they could do with an audience. Could all the family come? And maybe some friends too?"

Poppy sat in bed, thinking. She always felt great when she and Zack were bouncing around the floor in a Latin American samba, or circling it in a smooth ballroom dance like the foxtrot. The thought of being watched this afternoon by Mum, Dad and Auntie Jill, as well as Zack's mum, made her feel excited. Tom had agreed to come along, too. "Yay!" she said to herself.

The phone rang. Mum's head poked round

Poppy's bedroom door. "Mrs Porter wants to know if you'd like to go swimming with Mia this morning."

"Oh, yes, please!" exclaimed Poppy. "I haven't been swimming for *ages*!"

She couldn't stay in bed any longer. She put the CD player on and started to do one of her competition dances in front of the big mirror in her room. Dancing the cha-cha-cha in her pyjamas certainly looked funny!

"What's that racket?" called Dad's voice from the sitting-room.

"Too early, Poppy!" called Auntie Jill from her bedroom next to Poppy's.

"Give us a break, Pop!" called Tom, who was eating his breakfast in the kitchen. "We've got enough of that this afternoon!"

Mum put her head around Poppy's door again. "Better get dressed," she said. "They're picking you up in twenty minutes."

Poppy really enjoyed herself at the pool. The two girls played in the water for a long time. Although Poppy noticed that the skin on her fingers was wrinkled, she didn't want to stop. But Mia was beginning to shiver.

"I'm so cold!" she told Poppy. "Look, my nails are blue. And I've got such cold feet!"

So they got out of the pool, and after they'd changed they went to the pool café for strawberry milkshakes.

"Mia tells me you're working very hard at your dancing," said Mrs Porter, smiling at Poppy with her whole face. She was so tiny and delicate that she always reminded Poppy of a doll.

"Yes, Zack and I are practising for the Regional Championships," said Poppy, sipping her milkshake. "If we do well enough, we'll be able to enter the Nationwide Finals next year."

Mia's mum looked impressed. "You'd never think ballroom dancing needed so much work," she said. "The dancers make it look easy, and it's so beautiful to watch!"

A thought struck Poppy. "Would you like to come to our dress rehearsal this afternoon?" she asked. "You and Mia? Miss Johnson says we need an audience."

Mia was nodding excitedly, her damp black hair shaking all around her head. "Can we go, Mum?" she asked.

"I'd love to!" said Mrs Porter. "Thank you, Poppy. I've always wanted to see you and your partner dance. I think a boy of your age who's interested in ballroom dancing must be very unusual."

Poppy sipped some more of her milkshake, considering what was unusual about Zack. In most ways he was an ordinary boy. He played video games and knew the names of all the cars. He liked doing maths problems, just like Tom, though this wasn't necessarily a boy thing. He worried that his hair didn't always stick up or lie down just as he wanted it, and that he wasn't as tall as he'd like to be. He could be grumpy sometimes, too.

But on top of all this ordinariness, he *wasn't* ordinary.

"He's special," she told Mia's mum. "He loves dancing as much as I do. He's always practising and looking out for new steps, and he's just sort of ... nice."

"But if so few boys like dancing," said Mrs Porter thoughtfully, "are there enough boys for every girl to have a partner?"

Poppy shook her head. "No. Lots of girls have girl partners. I'm lucky to have Zack."

"Then boys like Zack must be as valuable as gold!" said Mrs Porter, smiling her big smile again.

Poppy sat between Tom and Auntie Jill in the back seat of Dad's car, clutching her dance bag on her knees. Auntie Jill held Poppy's

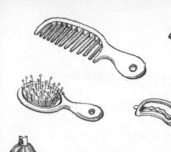

dress in its plastic cover, and Mum had already put make-up on Poppy's face and pinned up her hair. Poppy's tummy felt wobbly. What would it feel like, she wondered, when she was on her way to the *real* competition?

"You look tired, Poppy," said Mum, looking round from the front seat. "Maybe you shouldn't have gone swimming this morning."

"It was fun, though," said Poppy. "And it's great that Mia and her mum are coming to watch us dance this afternoon. I hope they like it."

"Dancers always dance better when they've got an audience," said Auntie Jill. "I know I used to."

When they got to
the dance school Mrs Porter and Mia
were already there. But there was no sign of
Zack, and Miss Johnson wasn't in the studio.

"She must be in the office," said Dad. "The
door's closed."

"Maybe Zack and his mum are stuck in
traffic," said Mum to Mrs Porter.

They all sat down on the chairs set out
around the edge of the studio and waited.
The wobbliness in Poppy's tummy got worse.
She knew something wasn't right, she just
knew it.

Then Miss Johnson came in. Her hair was in a ponytail and she was wearing a black flared skirt and flesh-coloured shoes, just like she always did, but her face was very serious. Poppy's heart began to jump about.

"That was Zack's mother on the phone," said Miss Johnson. "I'm sorry, but Zack isn't coming."

"Oh no! Is he ill?" asked Mum.

Miss Johnson took a deep breath before she spoke. "No, he's not ill. He says that after the Regionals he's going to give up dancing completely."

There was a silence. Poppy wasn't sure she'd heard correctly.

Auntie Jill put her hands over her cheeks. "Give up!" she gasped. "But why?"

"I don't really know," said Miss Johnson.

"He just says he doesn't want to have to worry about dancing any more. He'll do the Regionals, but Mrs Bishop says he refuses to come to this dress rehearsal. She's very upset."

Tears came into Poppy's eyes. The thought of Zack sitting at home worrying was enough to make her cry, but losing her partner was even worse. "Oh, poor Zack!" she said. "How can we change his mind?" She turned to Miss Johnson. "We must think of something!"

Miss Johnson put her hand on Poppy's shoulder. "You might as well go home," she said. "You can't do the rehearsal without Zack."

Poppy thought about Mia, and Mrs Porter, and Tom. She couldn't let them down. "No," she said to Miss Johnson, "but I *can* do it with *you*!"

She sounded so determined, Miss Johnson couldn't help smiling. "All right," she said, taking Poppy in a ballroom dance hold while their "audience" applauded. "You're not going to give up without a fight, are you, Poppy Love?"

It was Wednesday afternoon, before Competition Class. Poppy knew Zack always got to the studio early, as he came straight from school. Today she had asked Mum to take her early too, so she could talk to Zack before the others arrived.

"What is it, Zack?" asked Poppy as soon as she arrived. "You love dancing, so why don't you want to do it anymore?"

Zack put down his bag and looked at the studio floor.

"I do love dancing, Pop," he said, "but … I don't know, the thought of all those people watching us and clapping…"

Poppy remembered the applause at their first competition. "This feels so great!" Zack had said to her, with the biggest smile she'd ever seen on his face. So what he was saying now didn't make sense. Poppy waited while he thought.

"I can't let my mum down," he said. "She's got such hopes for me at school, it would be so awful if I failed."

"But what about Miss Johnson?" said Poppy. "Wouldn't it be letting *her* down if you give up dancing?"

Zack shook his head. "I don't care," he said. "I mean, I do care, but…" he stopped, wondering how to go on.

Poppy couldn't very well say "And what about me?", though she was thinking it. Without Zack, it would be hard for her to win a competition, ever.

"My mum's on her own, you see…" went on Zack.

Poppy nodded. Zack's mum and dad had split up a long time ago, when Zack was a baby. Since then, Mrs Bishop had looked after him without any help.

"So I think I should give up dancing and spend my time on my schoolwork," said Zack.

Poppy didn't know what to say. But then she had an idea. "Shall I tell you something?" she asked Zack. "It might help."

"I doubt it," said Zack gloomily. "But go ahead."

"Well, there's this boy at school called

Ryan, who thinks dancing is a complete joke. He doesn't tease Mia about her gymnastics, but he's always making fun of my dancing. He's really horrible sometimes."

Zack was looking straight at her. "And what do you do," he asked, "when he's horrible?"

"I ignore him," said Poppy. "It's hard sometimes, but I have to. If I answered him, it would just make him say worse and worse things."

The expression on Zack's face made Poppy realize what his real reason was for giving up dancing. She felt very sorry for him.

"Look," she said, "boys who pick on people should get into trouble. You can't let them get away with it."

Zack shook his head. "It's no use, Pop. There are too many of them ganging up on me. I hate football, but I'm going to have to start playing it."

Poppy thought hard, biting her lip. "We'll think of something," she said.

"I don't think we will." Zack sort of smiled. "I'm sorry, but I'm going to give up after the Regionals, and that's that."

Poppy didn't say anything. She felt like crying. But the studio was beginning to fill up with dancers doing their warm-up exercises, and she didn't want them to see that she was upset.

"Come on, we'd better get changed," said Zack, picking up his bag. Then he seemed to think of something, and looked carefully

at Poppy. "You won't tell anyone
about this, will you?"

"No, of course not," promised Poppy.

"What will you say when people ask
you why I gave up?"

Poppy hesitated. Then she
remembered that last Saturday at the
swimming pool, Mia had told Poppy that
she had cold feet. But there was another kind
of cold feet, which meant that someone had
changed their mind about something they
had to do, and tried to get out of doing it.

"It'll be all right," she told Zack. "I'll
just tell them something happened to you
that happens to everyone
sometimes, and not just
when they're swimming!
You got cold feet."

Zack nodded and pushed open the door to the corridor. Poppy watched him thoughtfully.

"Your feet might be cold right now, Zack Bishop," she said under her breath, "but I just *know* they'll warm up again. You won't give up. You love dancing too much!"

Famous for a Day

It was the day of the South East Regional Championships.

In the crowded changing room there was just enough space for Poppy to sit down and look in the mirror inside the lid of her make-up box. Her face looked pale and tired. Well, she had got up at six o'clock, and hadn't been able to sleep on the long drive from Brighton. And she'd been too nervous to eat any breakfast.

Mum hung up the new
dress Mrs Heatherington
had made especially for
this competition. It was
the palest green, with
a skirt that flared out
into a circle when
Poppy twirled. "Would
you do Poppy's tan when you've finished
her hair?" Mum said to Auntie Jill. "Then I'll
make a start on her make-up."

Poppy felt like a puppet, with someone
pulling her strings. "Put your arms out,"
instructed Auntie Jill, the can of spray-on tan
in her hand. "Now, turn them. Slowly."

When Mum was doing Poppy's eye
make-up, she got cross because Poppy kept

64

blinking. "Mum, it's impossible not to blink!" Poppy told her.

Although Poppy loved the grown-up look the tan and the make-up gave her, and she loved putting on her silver shoes and spotless white socks and the swingy, swirly dress, she was always glad when the getting-ready was over. Turning this way and that, swishing her skirt, she suddenly couldn't wait to start dancing.

"Miss Johnson's ready for you to run through your steps," said Auntie Jill, folding up Poppy's clothes. "So bring Lucky and let's go."

Zack was sitting in the main hall with his mum and Miss Johnson. Dad and Tom were there too.

When Poppy came in with Mum and Auntie Jill, Dad's eyes lit up. "You look gorgeous!" he said. "Come here and have a hug."

"As long as you don't spoil her make-up!" said Mum.

Poppy knew that she and Zack looked good. The pale green dress went well with her dark hair, and its skirt would swing out beautifully around her tanned legs when she danced. Zack was wearing black trousers, a white long-sleeved shirt and a black bow tie, because that was the rule for a competition. The clothes were perfectly pressed, and he'd got his hair just right. Poppy thought he looked polished, like a new car.

The competition was being held in a leisure centre in London. The dance floor was bigger than any Poppy had seen before.

It had to be, because there were also more dancers than ever before. There were dresses of every colour and style, and silver and gold shoes, and sparkly hair decorations in the girls' buns, twists and French braids. Everyone was practising their steps, swaying and spinning and bouncing their way around the floor.

Poppy and Zack went out to the middle of the dance floor with Miss Johnson. The first events were the Latin American dances, so they practised the cha-cha-cha, then the paso doble.

In the paso doble Zack had to act like a bullfighter, and strut the steps proudly. Miss Johnson made them do it again, as she wasn't satisfied with Zack's strutting the first time. Then they did the rumba and the jive, which was one of Poppy's favourite dances.

Zack was so easy to dance with! Poppy knew where his feet were going to go and what his arms were going to do, and she fitted in with his movements smoothly. On their side-by-side steps in the jive they were perfectly in time with each other. They had never danced so well.

Poppy felt mixed up, though. She was happy but she couldn't help also being sad. Was this really the last time she and Zack would dance together?

If Zack did leave the dance school, Poppy

would have to dance with either Luke or Sam, who were the only other boys in the Competition Class. But Cora and Sophie were their partners, so it wouldn't be fair to them. And if Zack could get teased by silly boys about his dancing, might this happen to Luke and Sam too? Would they want to give up?

Whichever way Poppy looked at it, it wasn't fair.

"Sevens are supposed to be lucky," Miss Johnson said as she pinned the number 177 on the back of Zack's shirt. Silently her face said, "Don't let me down, will you?" But aloud she said with a smile, "Time to face the music and dance!"

Poppy and Zack looked at each other, puzzled. "How can we do that?" asked Zack. "If we face the stage where the music's coming from the whole time, we won't be able to dance."

Miss Johnson's smile got wider. "It's just an expression," she explained. "It means 'face a challenge fearlessly'. It's the name of an old song, too – a real favourite for ballroom dancing."

"Come on, then, Zack," said Poppy. "Let's face the music!"

The competition started. Zack held Poppy's hand up high and they walked onto the floor. She could tell by his face that he was feeling as mixed up as she was.

He looked sideways at her.

"Don't worry, Pop, I'm cool," he said. "How about you?"

"I'm cool," said Poppy, feeling relieved.

They faced the challenge as fearlessly as they could, and danced well. So well, in fact, that they got through to the next round in each of their events.

"Remember," said Miss Johnson after the second round of the cha-cha-cha and jive, "to qualify for the Nationwide Finals you don't have to win, you just have to get through to the semi-final."

They waited at the edge of the floor for the numbers for the semi-final of the paso doble and rumba to be announced. Poppy wondered if everyone in the room could see her legs trembling under her skirt. Zack held her hand very tightly.

"Number one-seven-seven!" called the announcer.

Poppy heard Mum shriek, but she didn't turn round. She and Zack walked out proudly, and joined the other semi-finalists in the centre of the huge floor. When Zack turned to face her for the start of the paso doble, she thought she had never seen him look so happy. And yet he was determined to give this up for ever!

They didn't get through to the final of any of the events. But they reached the semi-final of two Latin American dances. Miss Johnson, her cheeks very pink, hugged them both. "Well done, well done!"

"Nationwide Finals, here we come!" yelled Zack excitedly. Then he remembered. "Oo-er..." he said, more quietly.

Auntie Jill rushed towards Poppy and Zack, her phone in her hand. "You've finished for now, haven't you?" she asked breathlessly. "Well, hurry up. Someone wants to meet you."

"Who?" asked Poppy.

"A reporter from the *Brighton Echo*," replied Auntie Jill.

Poppy's insides began to flutter a little. "But why has he come to see us?"

"Well…" Auntie Jill seemed embarrassed. "I knew him years ago, when I was a dancer. He heard that I was running a hotel in Brighton, and he thought it would make a good article for the newspaper. I told him about you and Zack doing this competition, so he's come here to interview you. He's waiting in the cafeteria."

Zack was fiddling with his hair and

frowning. "Are we going to be in the paper?" he asked. "I mean, are people really going to read about us?"

"Yes, they are," said Auntie Jill.

Zack, Poppy and Miss Johnson followed Auntie Jill to the cafeteria, where a man sat drinking coffee from a paper cup. He had a notebook and a camera, and on the table in front of him there was a tape recorder. Smiling, he stood up.

"This is Richard Cusson," said Auntie Jill. "Richard, meet Sarah Johnson. She runs the Blue Horizon Dance Studio."

The reporter shook Miss Johnson's hand. "May I call you Sarah?" he asked. "Please call me Richard."

"And this is my niece, Poppy Love, and her partner, Zack Bishop," said Auntie Jill.

Richard was quite young, and was wearing a baseball cap. He didn't look much like a reporter, Poppy thought.

"Hello, you two," he said. "Ready for the interview?"

Poppy and Zack looked at each other. "You bet!" said Zack, and everyone laughed.

"Right," said Richard as they sat down. "I'm doing this article for the *Echo* because these Regional Championships cover the Brighton area. I'll get some photos in a minute."

"Awesome!" exclaimed Poppy. "We'll be famous for a day!"

Richard Cusson nodded cheerfully. "Maybe for longer," he said. "Like Jill." He looked at Auntie Jill, then down at his notes. "Now, I'm going to tape our little chat." He adjusted the microphone and switched on the tape

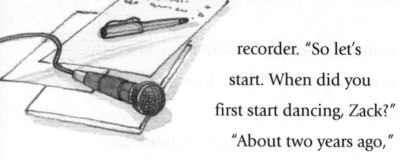

recorder. "So let's start. When did you first start dancing, Zack?"

"About two years ago," Zack said into the mike. "I was already in Miss Johnson's Competition Class when Poppy joined."

"Why did you want to do ballroom dancing?" asked Richard.

"Because I'm so terrible at football!" said Zack. Everyone laughed again. "And it just looked like fun to do," he added, going a bit pink.

"What about you, Poppy?" asked Richard.

"Um…" Poppy could hardly remember her life before dancing. "I'd seen it on TV and liked the dresses," she said. "I think."

"I see," said Richard, nodding. "But isn't

it also because you want to be as famous as your aunt? Follow in her footsteps – or dance steps, you might say?"

Poppy was so surprised she didn't say anything for a moment. She had never imagined she would ever be famous, even for one day. "Well … of course I want to be a champion dancer like my auntie, and Zack and I like entering competitions, don't we, Zack? But it's just for fun."

"I see." Richard consulted his notes. "This is going to be a very good story," he said to Poppy and Zack. "Thanks for speaking to me."

He closed his notebook, and was about to turn off the tape recorder when he remembered something. "Oh, one more thing," he said, holding the microphone in front of Poppy and Zack. "Jill tells me you've qualified for the Nationwide Finals. Are you intending to compete in that event? It's the highlight of the ballroom dancing year, I understand."

No one said anything. Everyone except Richard knew that because Zack had decided to give up dancing, he and Poppy wouldn't be entering the Nationwide Finals. But if the newspaper article was going to say how well they'd done today in the Regionals, might that make the boys at Zack's school realize that dancing needed talent, skill and practice, just like football? Most importantly, might they see that in both things – a football match and a dance competition – you had to try as hard as you could to make your team win?

Would Zack think about this too, and change his mind? Poppy held her breath.

"Well…" Zack began slowly, "if we've qualified for the Nationwide Finals, I suppose we might as well enter them." For the first time that day, Poppy saw his face break into a proper smile. "I mean, we want to do the best we can, don't we, Poppy?"

Poppy smiled too. "Yes, we do," she agreed. "And who knows, we might even end up being famous – for more than just one day!"

Natasha May loves dance
of all kinds. When she was a little girl
she dreamed of being a dancer, but also
wanted to be a writer. "So writing about
dancing is the best job in the world,"
she says. "And my daughter, who is
a dancer, keeps me on my toes about
the world of dance."

Shelagh McNicholas
loves to draw people spinning around
and dancing. Her passion began when
her daughter, Molly, started baby ballet
classes, "and as she perfected
her dancing skills we would practise
the jive, samba and quickstep
all around the house!"